Cherish

by

Emma Johnson Proctor

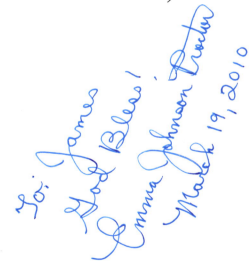

To: James
God Bless!
Emma Johnson Proctor
March 19, 2010

DORRANCE PUBLISHING CO., INC.
PITTSBURGH, PENNSYLVANIA 15222

ISBN # 0-8059-4248-3
Printed in the United States of America

First Printing

For information or to order additional books, please write:
Dorrance Publishing Co., Inc.
643 Smithfield Street
Pittsburgh, Pennsylvania 15222
U.S.A.

In loving memory of my mother, Mrs. Bessie (Weebie) Mays, who departed from this planet on December 4, 1993, and my grandmother, Mrs. Hilda (Nina) Williams, who departed from this planet on December 25, 1975.

You both are so very far away.
I think of you often, from day to day.
I know that you are sitting in heaven above
With God and Jesus there to love.
Surrounded by friends and loved ones, too.
I know that you are happy, but I really miss you.

Thanks for instilling in me to see
The love of God that He's given me.
Because if it had not been for the both of you,
I wouldn't be doing today what God wants me to.
You taught me about God when I was a tot.
Mistakes I did make, I made a lot.
But through it all, I turned out all right.
Because you place God within my sight.

I do thank you for all that you have done.
And when this battle on earth is won,
I'll meet you in that heavenly home,
Where you and other loved ones roam.

Until we meet again,

With love,

Your daughter and granddaughter

June 25, 1996

Contents

CHILDREN

Foreword

It was in Frankfurt and Hanau, Germany, when I really searched for God. That was about fifteen years ago. I have known of God all of my life. When I began to search, not just to know of Him, but to know Him personally, He began to manifest in my life in many ways. I began to seriously spend time with Him through prayer, Bible study, reading, meditation, and searching. I have been growing ever since. I moved from Germany to Indianapolis, Indiana, where my spiritual development continued to improve with more study, more prayer, more reading, more meditation, and more searching. I now live in Davidsonville, Maryland where I will continue on my Spiritual path.

I have learned what love really is. It is not what you get, but what you give. I have learned what forgiveness is, and what God meant when He said to "Bless your enemies." I have learned that when someone hurts you, it only hurts for a little while and that life and love must go on.

I have come to realize that Jehovah God is my first love and although I love others, He is my daily bread, my source, my protector, my Father, my friend. He and only He has never left or forsaken me. He fulfills my desires, my wants, my needs.

Although I love my fellow man, I am learning not to depend on human approval. I am learning that what I do in this life is to ask for God's approval, and that I must answer to Him and Him alone. He is the one that will help me to reach my eternal home.

God is everything and all to me. I place no one before Him. "Thank you, Jehovah, for my trials and tribulations, for they only bring me closer and closer to Thee."

I still have a lot of growing to do, but I know that as long as I keep my hands in God's hands, let Him guide me, keep my mind on Him and pray, He will never leave or forsake me.

Praise ye the Lord. Praise the Lord, O my soul.
Psalm: 146:1

Acknowledgements

Psalm: 121:1-2

I will lift up my eyes unto the hills from whence cometh my help.
My help cometh from the Lord which made heaven and earth.

This book is being dedicated to Jehovah God, for it was He that inspired me to write. I give all credit to Him for without Him, I can not do anything.

Thanks to my daughter and her husband—Regina and Marcus Bennett; and to friends Ramona Green and Alcelia Buck for their encouragement and assistance. Thanks to my mother, Mrs. Bessie Hayes Mays, who departed this life on December 4, 1993, and to my grandmother, Mrs. Hilda Clark Williams, who left this planet on December 25, 1975, for instilling in me the love of God. Thanks to my husband, my other children, my grandchildren, and my great grandson for their patience and love. And many thanks to everyone that is or was a part of my life, for had it not been for all of you and the role that you played in my life, today I might not be on my spiritual path.

Most of all, my thanks to You, Jehovah God.

GOD SO LOVED!

We should love too.

Family and Friends

I love you, I love you, I love you, I do!
May God bless each one of you.
For you are very close to my heart.
And you will always be a part
Of the love I try so hard to sow.
Now and forever more.
You will always be a part of me,
In this life and through eternity.

> May God Bless You with
> Peace,
> Love,
> Joy,
> And Your Ultimate Goal,
> Heaven

Friends

When God brings people together to be friends,
That friendship will last even when life ends.

You are a friend I have treasured so dear,
When I am away or when I am near.

God knows the kind of friends we need.
And I love you as a friend, indeed.

True friends are so hard to find,
I am glad God chose you as a friend of mine.

In my absence, when I was far away,
You were on my mind many a day.

You've gone in your directions, and I've had to go in mine, too.
Our friendship has weathered the storm that has kept me from you.

A friend is a person that you don't always have to see,
But still your friendship will always be.

As we walk this life's journey that one day will end.
May we walk with God together where the road does not bend.

I thank you, Ramona, for being a friend.

Sisterly Love

Our friendship could never be compared with another.
For God chose us to be sisters, though we have not the same mother.
For God does what He wants to do.
He made sisters of us, yes, we two.
You've been part of my life for many years.
We've shared much laughter and some tears.
We've shared a lot of secrets, too.
Yes, they have remained with me and you.
We raised our children and looked out for each.
We were always there within each other's reach.
We kept in contact when I was away.
Your sisterly love was there from day to day.
If not in person, then in heart.
Our sisterly love lasted even when we were apart.
You are my friend and my sister, it's true.
I'll always reach out to you.
If you need me, I'll be there.
Whether I am here or anywhere.
And when this life's journey someday will part
You'll remain, always, within my heart.
We will someday meet at the pearly gate,
Where God, Jesus, and loved ones wait.
I love you, sister, through all eternity.
We will walk in heaven, you and me.

We will sit with our Father, God above.
And tell Him about our sisterly love.
Even though we know He knew it from birth.
Way before we came to planet earth.
That we would be sisters and good friends.
And that, my sister, will never end.

Thank you for being my sister and friend,

With sisterly love,

Always.

July 3, 1996

Keep God Near

May God bless you each and every day.
I am sure He will show you the correct way.
To live this Journey of Life the way it should be.
Just let Him guide you and you will see.
That all things will turn out right
If you keep God within sight.
Keep Him in your hearts and minds
And everything will turn out fine.
Just keep Him with you wherever you go.
Always continue to love Him so.
Remember the love of God is there.
He will be with you everywhere.
And when this life someday will end.
He'll meet you where the road never bends

June 16, 1996

Thank You

I am a Christian and God loves me.
I am a Christian and that's what I wish to be.
I am not perfect, but thank God I am free.
I thank Him for saving a sinner like me.

October 15, 1996

Not Perfect

I am not perfect and don't claim to be.
I am still growing and pray that I see
The heavenly home above the bright sky
Where someday I hope to be, yes, by and by.
I will work hard to reach that heavenly shore.
Where sin will prevail no more.
My perfection on earth will never be.
But I'll pray and work hard for God to see.
That I love Him and will respect His word, it's true.
And will do my best to do what He wants me to.

November 16, 1996

Time

Time is at hand that we humans must take heed to the
direction that God has laid out for us.

It's not time for playing games, living lies, taking drugs,
stealing, killing, or even making a fuss.

This generation of people on earth is changing, they
seem to be getting bolder.

The young, I am afraid, are dying younger and the old
are getting older.

The time, it seems to be close; it's almost at the millennium.

The time, the Bible says that Jesus soon will come.

The folks on earth must get ready for the events that will
take place.

The time is now, to be close to God and to stay in God's
grace.

It's time to take things in stride and do the best that we can.

To treat everyone with kindness; to love every human.

The time will come when we must answer to God for the things we do on earth,

When we get to our heavenly home, in the heavenly bounded turf.

The time is now, while we are here, to make peace with God and man,

For those of us who wish to live in the heavens of heavenland.

Time is running out, people, so let us get together.

So we can flock in our heavenly home like birds of a feather.

February 1, 1996

Forgiveness

Let's cleanse our hearts with forgiveness, for we can not carry unforgiveness into the kingdom of Heaven. Everyone and everything there, will be on one accord.

There will be love in Heaven for everyone to see.
Much peace, joy, and tranquility.
Everyone has at one time hurt someone.
It's now time for unforgiveness to be undone.
If God had not forgiven us, where would we be today?
We would not be walking towards the "King's Highway."
So let the unforgiveness go.
And let the love begin to flow
Before we leave this earthly sod.
For all have come short of the glory of God.
Forgiveness is the way to be happy and free.
That's the way God wants us all to be.

February 12, 1995

Christian Walk

I have no time for people talk.
My time is now for my Christian Walk.
To do what God wants me to.
To love everyone as He would do.
I am not perfect and don't claim to be,
But pray that God will let me see
The way to love my fellow man
While I am living upon this land.
For now I live for Christ alone.
Until I reach my Heavenly home.

January 22, 1996

He's Everything

God is the maker of the sun, moon, and stars.
He is the maker of Jupiter, Venus, and Mars.
He is the maker of everything you see.
Including the birds, animals, and bees.
He's our creator, our friend, and Father, too.
He's everything to me and to you.
He's the sunshine, He's the rain.
He's always there to share our pain.
He loves us more than we'll ever know.
He's always with us and teaches us to grow.
He's the creator, the creator of all.
He's there to catch us when we fall.
He's our Father God above.
Who's always there to give us love.

October 22, 1996

Invite Him In

God is our all and all.
He is there to hear our every call.
He is the God that lives above.
He is always near to give His love.
He is omnipresent, that means He's everywhere.
He is omnipotent, "Our God," He really cares.
He will always, always see us through.
No matter what we say or do.
Just invite Him to come in.
He will always be there to be your friend.
Just call on Him and He will come
To you, to me, to everyone.

November 1, 1996

Angels

Heavenly Angels are with us today.
God sends His messengers to show us the way.
They are beautiful, if we could only see.
They are sent to guide you and me.
They can travel to earth from heaven above.
They are sent from God with everlasting love.
They are here and sometimes we don't realize,
Because we can't always see them with our eyes.
We can hear them with our ears if we listen carefully.
They are the inner voices that tell us where to go or where not to be.
They will be with us until this earthly life ends.
They are our guardians and our friends.
And even through eternity
They will always be with you and with me.

December 15, 1996

Keep an Open Mind

"God moves in mysterious ways."

God tries to get our attention to get us ready for the coming of Jesus Christ. Sometimes He tries through a trial, through a tribulation, through reading, through ministers, through evangelists, through prayer, and yes, sometimes through each other.

We should keep open minds because an open mind is a way of learning and a closed mind learns nothing.

December 1, 1996

God, What Will You Have Me to Do?

Acts: 9:6 says, "Lord, What will thou have me to do," and the Lord said, "Arise, go into the city, and it shall be told thee what thou must do."

When God sends you someplace, it may not be where you want to go and it may not be where someone else thinks you should go, but you go anyway.

When God leads you to do something, it may not be something that you want to do and others might feel that you shouldn't do it, but you do it anyway.

When God tells you to speak about something, it may not be what you want to say and surely it might not be what someone wants to hear, but you say it anyway.

When you pray and ask God where you should go, what you should do, or what you should say, and the answer is given, all should listen.

February 18, 1996

Battle Not Won

Thank you, God, for all that You have done.
As You know, the battle for me on earth is not yet won.
But I know that You are my guiding light to the end.
And sooner or later this battle I will win.
The battle of this life can be chaotic and cruel
Without You being my guiding tool.
For without You, I could not exist.
Thank You for being in my midst.
Thank You for Your kind and everlasting love.
Thank You, my true friend and Father above.

December 2, 1996

He Gives All

May the love of God bring peace to our minds, love to our hearts, and abiding grace within us.

Remember God first in your life for His love will endure forever.

All things belong to the Master of the Universe, Father of us all. He has loaned us all that we have. Our children do not belong to us; they are His. The houses, clothes, cars, money, etc. that we claim that we own, are His. Without Him we would have nothing. We would be nothing. We must understand these things. We came into this world with nothing, so be it, that we will leave this world without anything.

We are spiritual beings in these physical bodies. God gave us these bodies to be able to live on planet Earth, to learn to get to higher levels of consciousness (higher levels of learning) to be able to "know" Him, not just to know of Him. Also to know that we are one with Him and all mankind. For we are here to learn to love as He loves, for God himself is love.

Yes, we are one with our Father God. When we humans realize this, we will have the peace we so often seek, the help we so often need, the true love we so desire, and the strength to endure.

July 13, 1995

Satan Can Do No Harm

When you know that you are close to God, don't ever feel that Satan and his army can do you any harm. God is your protector. He will protect you from all snares of the enemy.

Satan and his army will sometimes come upon you.
And sometimes you won't know what to do.
They will hit where you really don't want them to hit.
There where your future and loved ones sit.
Whether it's your job, school, or family,
They are there for many, yes, many to see.
They will come to you with force, it's true.
God told you in Ephesians, Chapter 6, just what to do.
Remember, God is the master and He has the master plan.
He'll soon eradicate Satan and his army from this land.
And all will be peaceful and all will be free.
Satan and his army will never more be.

December 22, 1995

Growth

When I was just a little girl, I didn't understand.
A lot of things that I do now, since I've lived in this land.
I've had a chance to live, and I've had a chance to grow.
To grow means maturity, to live in the flow.
When one grows up it doesn't mean that one grows big and tall.
It means that one grows spiritually, it doesn't mean being big at all.
It means that one can comprehend why God has placed him here.
And why God gives His hand for you, to always feel Him near.
It means that one will understand God's word as He say.
God's word, I mean the Bible that will show one the way.
Yes, when one grows spiritually, he will be one
With the "Word," the beloved "Word," God's only son.
You see the "Word" is Jesus, and God's word is the Bible.
God holds us to His word, it's true, yes we are liable.
When one has learned these things in life, he will really know
What growing is, really is, and what it takes to grow.
It means that one can look at the past and know it had to be.
To grow, I don't mean big and tall, but to grow spiritually.

October 10, 1987

God's Way

Life on this planet sometimes gets rough.
Life on this planet sometimes gets tough.

As long as we know that God's love is here.
We never should feel any fear.

God said to be "in the world, not of it."
If we learn God's way, we'll know where we fit.

While on this planet, learn what you can
From God's teaching and not by man's.

For God is the giver, the giver of all,
And man's way is the way to let yourself fall.

But through it all, life can be sweet,
When you let God do the driving, and you take the seat.

June 1996

The Kingdom

The kingdom of heaven is a place we would all like to go.
But before we can get there, I am telling you, we all have to grow.
The kingdom is not for sinners, like you or me.
We have to get things together for God to see.
That we are trying to do our very, very best.
To get to the place where there is much peace and rest.
Don't take it lightly, but place it heavy upon your hearts.
That we must be ready in order to part
To the heavenly shore where peace will abide.
Where man will be free to never more hide.

February 1, 1996

Man's Laws

We are the people who can fight against wars.
Why can't we fight against man-made laws?
Man's laws are what causes things to be bad.
And that's why the world is so down and so sad.
He took the prayers out of the schools.
Man has let himself become such a fool.
He has let bad things take control.
Man in ruining his very soul.
He is ruining planet Earth as you can see.
He's not following God's laws as God would have him be.
He's ruining his own body and his own spiritual self.
All man is looking for is fame, fortune, and wealth.
As long as he's keeping his own laws, it's true.
He's keeping God's laws far away from you.
But *we can* fight so this world can be won.
By God's laws and the laws of Jesus, his son.
For God laid all the laws down to man.
But man has taken God's laws from this land.
Nothing will be right until God's laws come into play.
For these are the laws that will show man the way.
The way to saving his very own soul.
And that's when man will meet his ultimate goal.

June, 1996

What Do We See?

When we look at the heavens, what do we see?
Do we see the reflection of where we'd like to be?
Maybe the sun that gives us heat and makes things grow.
Maybe the moon that gives us light to guide where we like to go.
Maybe we see beyond the sky.
Where many, many mansions lie.
Maybe a planet away from the earth.
Where man is waiting to hit the turf.
Maybe we visualize the heaven above.
Where God and Jesus are there with much, much love.

November 10, 1996

God's Love

We humans use the *In-Love* words so often. We should eradicate these words from our vocabulary. God uses the word Love. Love is a word to be used to Love everyone. To be *In-Love* with anyone is a hurting process, because we earthlings place that person on a high level. God said, "Have no other gods before me." He said, "To *love* your neighbor as thyself." Parents *love* your children. Children, *love* your parents. Husbands, *love* your wives. Wives, *love* your husbands. "*Love* one another." Love is the magic word to be used. Love in the heart and soul is the key to peace and happiness.

Leave that emotional feeling of being *In-Love* out of your minds and hearts. These are words of hurt, fear, regression, lack of spiritual growth, depression, etc. We must use the word love and grow to love one another in a spiritual way. We are not here on this planet to idolize anyone. We are here to grow spiritually. To grow in that direction, we must not place emphasis of Love on any one individual and place him or her higher than our Creator, God.

When we are what we humans call *In-Love*, we seem to focus our minds and attentions on the one we are so-called *In-Love* with. If we would only focus our minds and attentions on our Creator, the Creator of the Universe, God, as we focus on the *In-Love* situation, we would find ourselves as to whom we are, where we have been, and where we are headed.

God is where our very beginning came from and He will be where the end of our being will advance. We must love one another, for we are a whole unit. For God created us all. No man, woman, or child can give us the love that God has for us. We have the ability to overcome the obstacles of this life. We must seek the way of overcoming our life situations that we created for ourselves. We can only do this through the Creator of the universe, our Father, our true, kind, loving, forgiving Father, God! We can endure. We can find peace and happiness.

Seek first the Kingdom of God and all things will come into focus. We will then know that no earthly being can make us happy. Happiness comes from within. God is that happiness. He is within each of us. He is the vine, we are the branches. He is the Creator, we are His creation. We can endure. With His help we most certainly can endure.

Let's place our priorities where they should be. First things first. "God" is first. We will overcome, because with God all things are possible. Remember the key word is "Love," "L-O-V-E". Love for God, love for self, love for family and love for your fellow man. For GOD'S LOVE, as He teaches, is the greatest love of all!

February 26, 1996

He's All I've Needed

The Lord has guided me into the direction that was best for me. When I wanted for something He gave me all I needed. He has made me lie in pastures of hope and dreams and guided me beside the water of life trials. He was there all the time. He restored into me the way into the kingdom of heaven. When I die, I know He will be with me. I have no fear of death. He will comfort me in this life and into the transition of the next life. Goodness will follow me because I will dwell in God's word, forever.

January 1996

Your Choices

When you are a child, it is by the teaching of God's word that your parents are to teach you in the way that you should go. When you become of age, you are then responsible for your own choices in life. Do not blame others for your mistakes. God has everything in the Bible that you need to know about the way you should live and the right choices to make. Keep His teachings close to you and read them daily.

God also has His messengers, His heavenly angels, here to guide you. You must listen very carefully to that inner voice that tells you what is right and what is wrong. Take the time to listen to your first instinct, then proceed to do what your heart and mind tells you. The angels will only guide you, you must listen carefully.

Your choices and not your circumstances determine your destiny. Disobedience produces disappointment and disappointment produces pain. God is willing to guide you, but you must choose the direction.

December 26, 1995

Think!

Most of us have been out in the world either one time or another.
Why then do we gossip and criticize our sisters and brothers?
Some are still out there.
And some have become aware
That God is totally the way to go.
And that we will definitely reap what we sow.
We have come in knowing where we have been.
Praying that there are things that we just won't do again.
But there are others, knowing what they have done and still do.
Are gossiping, criticizing, and hurting others, too
These same people that gossip and criticize
To God are not being very wise.
For God wants us to love each other
And not to hurt our sisters and brothers.
If there's anyone that can cast the first stone.
If there is, I am sure that you will stand alone
At the time when Judgment will take place.
You'll surely know that you're not in God's grace.
Because you have not loved, but have gossiped and criticized.
And have hurt others by telling many lies.
Why not try lots of love and lots of giving?
And you'll find that life will be worth living.
Not to live to gossip and criticize.
But to look at oneself and really surmise.
That the rules that God laid down for us to do.
Is to "do unto others as you would have them do unto you."

June 1996

29

Judge Not

Why are you judged for things you have done
And not for your growth since your victory was won?
Without mistakes, how would you know
What it takes in order to grow?
God knew mistakes were to be in.
He knew man would encounter great sin.
That's why He sent his Son to the cross
So humankind would not be lost.
So judge not, for we all do sin.
It's what's taking place in your heart that wins.
God will judge your heart, it's true.
So judge not, for it's up to God to do.

November 25, 1996

Love

Love is the answer to good health, good wealth, and good living.
Try love and try a lot of giving.
See what God will give back to you.
He will give all that you want Him to.
Love is the answer for all things on earth and above.
For God knows what He speaks of when He speaks about love.
Remember that love is the answer to all.
If man knew God's love, he would never have let himself fall.
God's love is placed in His word as He teaches.
It really is there within man's reaches.
So practice love for what you desire.
It takes love to get the things that you require.
Love is the answer to all good things.
Remember to practice love and see what it brings.

June 17, 1996

As You Travel

As you travel along the earthly plane,
One important thing for you to gain
Is to learn to love as God would have you do.
Also, to learn to help others, too.
Always take the time to see
The good in others and let them be.
For all have faults as we know,
But it takes love for each to grow.
Travel in God's light and in His love,
For that's what our God wants for us, that lives above.

December 15, 1996

Let Go and Learn

Don't you think its time for us
To let go of the bad things and the fuss?
So when Judgment Day does take place
We'll be able to meet God face to face.
And say to God, I have lived on earth with much
    chaos and turmoil.
But *thank you*, I've reached the heavenly soil.
Because I've read Your true word
And listen to the things I've heard.
To learn to reach the heavenly shore.
Where chaos and turmoil will be no more.

November 23, 1996

Mysteries

As I look to the heavens, I see the bright stars.
The wonders of God do I see.
I visualize Venus, Jupiter, and Mars,
And the vast universe there, forever to be.
I wonder what's really all that is out there.
Do you think one day I will know?
I believe there are many mansions out there, somewhere.
A mansion, someday I will go.
For as the earth sits out into space.
The sun and the moon sit there, too,
And all that someday that I must face
Will surely be many things out there, it's true.
For God one day will reveal it all.
Everything that's a mystery to me.
He'll explain why man let himself fall.
And the universe, He'll take me to see.

December 12, 1996

Our Duty to God

Our duty to God is to love everyone unconditionally.
That's what he wants from you and me.
He tells us to lay down our lives for our brothers.
All He is telling us is to love each other.
If we would only love like God wants us to.
We wouldn't be hurting others as we do.
The hatred, wars, drugs, rape, etc. would not take place.
We would all stay close to God and stay in His grace.
For loving is the only way to make it through.
To the heavens, where God sits and waits for me and for you.

November 1, 1996

Never More to Roam

Earth is a planet sitting out from the sun
Where man has been placed and not just for fun.
It is a place that we all should know.
It is a planet we came here only to grow.
To grow in order to get back from whence we came.
From the land of peace and the home of the tame.

For God our Father has sent us here.
To learn, to love, and not to fear.
It is a place where we reap what we sow.
That we will learn to sow no more
The bad things in life to keep us down.
From the heavenly shores where we are bound.

Sometimes I think that we come to the planet that
    sits out from the sun
To perfect the wrongs that we have done.
To please the Father, the Master of all
So we can be placed in the midst of the call.
The call that God says, "Child, come home."
The call from planet Earth, never more to roam.

February 1, 1996

The Trinity

There are three that are important for all of us to know.
We have to love each of them in order for us to grow.
If it had not been for God who gave His only begotten son,
Jesus, that bore our sins, so victory could be won,
The Holy Ghost that was sent to lead us into
All truth and understandings.
Just think, what would have happened to all of our sins?
We must thank the Father, the Son, and the Holy Ghost.
The Trinity, the three that love us, gave and gives the most.
And as we pray, let us look upon the sacred cross,
Realizing, had it not been for the three, all would be lost.
And as we look towards the heavens above,
Let us never to forget their precious love.

December 30, 1995

The Awakening

I see the pearly gates of heaven open wide.
I see lots of loved ones and friends inside.
I see God and Jesus with them.
And the Angels are singing beautiful hymns.
I see only the bright, bright light.
I see no darkness of the night.
I see the streets that are paved with gold.
I am standing there begging God to save my soul.
I see the wall built with precious stones
Of all sizes and all color tones.
I see no evil entering there.
Only love, laughter, and joy everywhere.
I see a river of pure Water of Life.
I see no turmoil, chaos, or strife.
I see my God sitting on the throne.
I am begging, "Please God, don't let me stand alone."
You see, I am dreaming and I am looking in
At a "real world" with no turmoil or sin.
I am awakening now, and now I see
That the dream that I dreamed will surely be.

Protection

The phrase has been used, "If it's not broken, don't fix it." No, you don't fix something that's not broken, but you do protect it.

If it's a marriage or relationship, you want to keep working at it
   so that it will last.
Try not working at it and it will soon pass.
If it's a crystal vase, you want to place it someplace where it
   won't fall.
If you don't protect it, you won't have it at all.
If it's a diamond, you'll protect it, you do
By keeping it very close to you.
If it's your family, you should protect it, too.
By doing what God has told each of His children to do
Is to love one another before it's too late.
Keep the family together with much love and no hate.
No, you don't fix something that's not broken, but you do
   protect it, you see.
For that's what you do and it will always be.
But protect it not, and let it go.
You'll find one day, it will be no more.

December 12, 1996

Let Love Flow

I have been and I am currently going through trials and tribulations for I am still growing spiritually. However, I have learned that my happiness comes from within. God is my happiness.

You and I must learn to listen very carefully to that inner voice that is within us. We must give more time to Meditation, Bible Study, and Prayer. We must learn to forgive those that have hurt us. We must learn to love everyone unconditionally.

No, we are not perfect. All have faults. But we must seek, ask, and knock. As the Bible says, "Seek and ye shall find." "Ask, and it shall be given to you." "Knock, and the door will be open."

I will, I know I will, until I leave this planet Earth, I will seek, ask, and knock. My mind will always be receptive to learning the way into the kingdom of Heaven. God's Kingdom which constitutes unconditional Love. "God is Love." How about you? You are part of God. Will you let love flow from your heart?

May God Bless You Abundantly,

September 20, 1996

CHILDREN

The Zoo

I was at the zoo the other day, and guess what I saw there?
I saw the elephant, snakes, and the big brown bear.
I also saw the turtle; he was sitting in the mud.
I saw the old gray goat; she was chewing on her cud.
I walked on by the goat, and guess what I saw?
I saw a great big tiger, licking his paw.
The big eagle with his wings as wide as can be
Seemed to be staring at little old me.
The giraffe with his neck so long, leaning on the fence.
Gave me goose bumps and made me a little tense.
The seal was there as I recall,
Having fun with the big, red ball.
The peacock was so pretty, as pretty as can be.
And there were many more animals there to see.
But time had passed me by and I was ready to go.
I had to come back again once more
To see the animals that I missed that day.
Including the pig, the lion, and the pretty blue jay.

June 29, 1988

Kids Have Gone Crazy

Some kids have gone crazy in the world of today
Because they don't listen to what their parents have to say.
Is it their parents who are really to blame?
Or is it society that has brought on the shame?
Society has placed values where they shouldn't be:
The drugs, the guns, the pornography.
Parents, we all are a part of this society.
We must plant our roots so the children can see
That we owe one another much respect
And that we are really here to project
The love of God, and then they will know
That love and kindness is the way to go.
Not the snorting, the killing, nor the nakedness,
But to grow to love and to do their best.
Please, parents, instill in our children the way back to the Lord.
The Master of the universe, Our Father, God.

February 6, 1996

See What I Saw

As I sit under the walnut tree
I am looking at the garden in front of me.
I sit here and as the birds fly by,
I see the corn stalks begin to die.
You see, the squirrels ate most of the corn.
They ate it at dawn, the beginning of morn.
The spinach that was there was planted for us,
Was eaten by rabbits with little or no fuss.
I looked at the mulberry tree; the berries are gone.
I see a little bird there singing a song.
The clouds are just moving, they are passing on by
As I look and see a jet plane up in the sky.
As I focus my eyes towards the green grapevine,
I can imagine the grapes becoming very good wine.
I see the scarecrow, he looks as tired as can be.
He didn't do his job well, as I see.
I turned my head and what did I see.
The big pear tree in back of me.
The cherry tree stands across from the pear.
The birds had eaten all the cherries from there.
As my eyes centers on the house in the middle of all
My mind goes back to really recall
The big walnut tree that I am sitting upon
Surrounded by shade, away from the sun.
I think of my God, the giver of all
And wonder why man let himself fall.
And I do thank God for all I can see.
And the wisdom and knowledge He has given to me.
And I do thank Him for the big walnut tree.
For that's where I was when I saw all I could see.

The Rod

You spoil the child by sparing the rod.
These are not my words, they are our Father, God's.
The rod is spared because of man's laws.
That's why we encounter many, many flaws
In our system of living in this world of today.
Because we won't follow God's laws that will show us the way,
The way that teaches us and our children what is right.
The things that are good for us and look good in God's sight.
If we start from the cradle and teach God's way of living,
Our lives here on earth would be of love and of giving.
God wants us all to be taught in the right way.
So we can look up to Him from each day to day.
And say, "God, we are doing what You have us to do.
We are teaching our children what You want us to."
So when they are grown, they will be good women and men.
They won't be dealing in corruption and sin.
For they had been taught that the rod wasn't spared.
And that God's laws are right, that He really cares.

May 9, 1996

Our Responsibility

People, God knows it's our responsibility
For all adults to actually see
That children must be children first.
And we are not here to teach them the worst.
If every adult would walk in the light,
And teach little children what is right,
They would learn about good and not about bad.
This world then wouldn't be so sad.
Let us keep our hearts aglow.
And teach our children the direction to go.

December 22, 1995

Take Care of the Children

The children belong to God up above
And they were placed here on earth to be loved.
They were not placed here to be abused
Or to be misguided or misused.

All adults are here to teach children how to live and how to love.
To teach them about their heavenly Father above,
So they can make it through the pearly gates
Where God and Jesus someday will wait.

People, take good care of the children as Jesus wants you to.
If you don't, you'll pay the price for what you didn't do.

June 25, 1996